grandma joins the All Blacks

HELEN M^CKINLAY • ILLUSTRATED *by* CRAIG SMITH

HarperCollins*Publishers*

ALL BLACKS is a registered trademark of the New Zealand Rugby Union
Incorporated and is used in this book with their kind permission.

National Library of New Zealand Cataloguing-in-Publication Data

McKinlay, Helen, 1947-
Grandma joins the All Blacks / Helen McKinlay ; illustrated by Craig Smith.
ISBN 978-1-86950-640-7
1. All Blacks (Rugby team)—Fiction. [2. Rugby Union football—Fiction. 3. Grandmothers—Fiction. 4. Humorous stories.]
I. Smith, Craig, 1955- II. Title.
NZ823.3—dc 22

First published 2007
Reprinted 2008 (twice), 2010, 2011 (three times), 2013
HarperCollins*Publishers (New Zealand) Limited*
P.O. Box 1, Auckland

ISBN: 978 1 86950 640 7

Cover design by Murray Dewhurst
Typesetting by Worksight Design

Printed in China by RR Donnelley

On Monday morning, Grandma woke up at six o'clock. She put in her false teeth,
dusted her wrinkles with her big feather duster and dressed in her granny clothes.
'Hmm,' she said. 'I think I'll make marmalade.'
'Miaowl,' said Scratch.

Grandma waved the wooden spoon.
'Tee hee,' she tootled. 'I'm going to be a good granny today.'

On Tuesday morning, Grandma woke up at seven o'clock. She put in her teeth, pulled on her tracksuit and dusted her wrinkles.

'Woo hoo,' she sang. 'Today I'm going to watch the All Blacks.'

She jumped on her skateboard and set off.

At the stadium she sat in the front row and took out her knitting.
'Knit one, purl one, knit one, purl one, knit one.'
The scarf grew and grew but the rugby field was empty.
'I think I'll investigate,' said Grandma.

There was a loud noise in the changing room.
'Boo,' it went and 'hoo' and 'boohoohoo'.

And there were the All Blacks blubbing and wiping their noses on their sleeves.
'What's the matter, boys?' asked Grandma.
'We don't want to play today, Gran,' they howled.
'Don't be silly,' she said. 'There's a test match on Saturday.
You have to practise.'

'We're tired of practice,' they sobbed.
'Hmm,' she hmmed. 'You need some of my marmalade.'
She took a jar out of her handbag and gave them each a teaspoonful.

They perked up straight away and jogged out to the field.
Grandma trotted behind waving her rugby scarf.
'Hurrah for the All Blacks,' she cried.

When they had finished, she made them a cup of tea.

'Well done, boys,' she said. 'I'll be off now.'

'Bye, Gran,' waved the All Blacks. 'Thanks for the marmalade.'

Grandma did a wheelie in the car park and whizzed home for lunch.

On Wednesday morning, Grandma woke up at eight o'clock.
She dusted her wrinkles and put in her teeth.
'I think I'll plant vegetables today,' she said.
The phone rang. It was the All Black coach.

'Good morning, Gran. The team won't get out of bed. What shall I do?'

'Ah ha,' said Grandma. 'They need a break. I'll take them rafting.'

'Can I come?' asked the coach.

'Of course,' said Grandma.

'Just give me half an hour
in the garden.'

She put on her wetsuit and flippers and went to plant cabbages.
When the All Blacks arrived, she flip flopped onto the bus. 'Let's go ride the rapids, boys,' she said.

That night, Grandma fell asleep in her chair.
She was still wearing her wetsuit.

On Thursday morning, Grandma woke up at nine o'clock. There was a knock on the bedroom window. It was the All Blacks. She put her teeth in quickly.
'Come in,' she called. They climbed in one by one.

'Good morning, Gran. We've brought you breakfast in bed. Bagels and bacon.'

'Mmm mmm,' said Grandma.

She patted the quilt. 'Sit down, boys,' she said.

'Where are we going today, Gran?' they asked.
'I haven't dusted my wrinkles yet but how about the circus? We could ride the dodgems
and do a spot of tightrope walking.'

'Yippee,' cheered the All Blacks. 'We'll do the dishes while you get dressed.'
'Oh you are kind,' said Grandma.
She dusted her wrinkles and put on her circus outfit.

When the last All Black leapt off the tightrope,
Grandma clapped her hands.
'I'm hungry. Let's get fish and chips.'
'Right,' said the coach. 'My treat.'
Everyone rubbed their tummies.
'Yum,' they said.
Grandma drove the bus home that night.

On Friday morning, Grandma woke up at ten o'clock. She hummed to herself in the shower as she scrubbed her wrinkles and rinsed her teeth. A text message tinkled on her mobile.

'Hi, Gran,' it said. 'We've got practice. Hope you can make it.'

Gran texted back, 'On my way.'

She put on a shirt and shorts, popped an extra jar of marmalade in her handbag and hopped on her scooter. She was just in time to join the haka.

That night she had dinner early and sat down to finish her rugby scarf.

On Saturday, Grandma woke up at eleven o'clock. She dusted her wrinkles, put in her teeth and made a pot of tea.

'Bee boppa do da,' she danced. 'I'm going to watch the test match.'

She put on her best dress and the hat with the red roses on and rang a taxi.

The coach met her at the stadium gate.
'Thank goodness you're here, Gran,' he said.
'The Captain's gone home with chickenpox.'
The All Blacks were very glum.

'Come along now, boys,' said Gran.
'A tablespoon of marmalade and you'll be just fine.'
They perked up marvellously.

'Gran for Captain! Gran for Captain!' they shouted.

'I'll need a uniform,' said Grandma.

'Come with me,' said the coach.

Grandma put on her All Black clothes and straightened her hat. Then she slipped her teeth into her handbag, in case they fell out in the scrum, and led the team onto the field.

Grandma scored the first try. She grabbed the ball and ran and ran and ran and ran.

She was home late that night.
There was a big party.

On Sunday morning, Grandma woke up at twelve o'clock. She dusted her wrinkles, put in her teeth and went to the spa pool.

When she got home there was a queue of reporters at her door. They asked her lots of questions.

'All in a day's work,' said Grandma.

On Monday morning, Grandma woke up at six o'clock. She put in her teeth, dusted her wrinkles and went downstairs for breakfast.

'Hmm. Not one jar of marmalade left,' she said.

She picked up the phone.

'Good morning. Is that the All Blacks? Captain Gran here. I need you to come and help make marmalade.'

And they did.